Pony Club Weekend

www.**kidsatrandomhouse**.co.uk
www.**katiesperfectponies**.co.uk

Katie Price's Perfect Ponies

1. **Here Comes the Bride**
2. **Little Treasures**
3. **Fancy Dress Ponies**
4. **Pony Club Weekend**

PONY CLUB WEEKEND
A BANTAM BOOK 978 0 553 82077 5

First published in Great Britain by Bantam,
an imprint of Random House Children's Books
A Random House Group Company

This edition published 2007

1 3 5 7 9 10 8 6 4 2

Mixed Sources
Product group from well-managed
forests and other controlled sources
www.fsc.org   Cert no. TT-COC-2139
© 1996 Forest Stewardship Council

Set in 14/21pt Bembo MT Schoolbook

Bantam Books are published by Random House Children's Books,
61–63 Uxbridge Road, London W5 5SA

www.kidsatrandomhouse.co.uk
www.rbooks.co.uk

Addresses for companies within The Random House Group Limited
can be found at: www.randomhouse.co.uk/offices.htm

THE RANDOM HOUSE GROUP Limited Reg. No. 954009
A CIP catalogue record for this book is available from the British Library.

Printed in the UK by CPI Bookmarque, Croydon, CR0 4TD

Pony Club Weekend

Illustrated by Dynamo Design

Bantam Books

Vicki's Riding School

Vicki

Jess and Rose

Cara and Taffy

Amber and Stella

Sam and Beanz

Mel and Candy

Henrietta and President

Darcy and Duke

Chapter 1

Cara sat on her bed with its pretty pink pony duvet. Holding a piece of paper in one hand and a pencil in the other, she ticked off each item on her list.

"Jodhpurs, jeans, pink hoodie with sparkly pony on the front, blue hoodie with sparkly pony on the front, three T-shirts, vest, knickers, socks and pyjamas. Wellies, cagoule, body protector, hot-water bottle, sleeping bag." Suddenly she stopped reading out loud and jumped up. "Hah! Forgot my trainers!"

Pulling back her long blonde hair so that it didn't fall into her eyes, Cara rooted around under the bed. Smiling with relief, she pulled out the trainers, wrapped them in a plastic bag and dropped them into her bulging rucksack. As she tried to fasten it, her eyes fell on two photographs by her bed.

One was a picture of Taffy, a beautiful palomino Welsh pony with a creamy blond mane and tail.

The other was of Cara with her dad, taken before the terrible car crash that killed him. Cara's eyes stayed on the photograph of Dad laughing and cuddling her. Even after a year she still couldn't believe that he was really gone.

After Dad's accident she and her mum had totally relied on each other and it felt like their whole world had been destroyed. Ever since his death they'd hardly been apart. The pony club weekend was going to be Cara's first time away from home and she was feeling really nervous.

Cara had never ridden when her dad was alive. She'd always loved animals, especially little ponies, but she'd been afraid of riding. However, it was during those horrible months just after her dad's death, when Cara hardly left the house, that her mum had suggested she do something new and had taken her to Vicki's stables. Cara had been so nervous she'd cried in the car and her mum had pulled over to give her a hug.

"You can't mope around for ever, sweetheart. You know your dad wouldn't have liked that," Mum had said gently. "Life has to go on. You've got to start living. That's what Dad would have wanted."

Tears had filled Cara's big blue eyes but she'd nodded in agreement. "You're right, Mum. It's totally what Dad would have wanted."

So Cara had got over her fear and gone to Vicki's Riding School, and after just one visit life had already seemed better. She

loved all the ponies there – pretty Rose,
a grey Connemara; gentle Stella, a black
Highland pony with a white blaze; crazy
Beanz, a skewbald New Forest cross; and a
stunning little chestnut Arab called Candice,
who was nicknamed Candy.

But Cara's favourite pony was Taffy.
When she first saw the cute palomino, her
heart had just melted. Taffy had whinnied
softly and moved towards her but Cara was
nervous and stepped away. Taffy wasn't
taking no for an answer though. Sensing
her fear, he'd gently rubbed his velvety soft
nose against her arm and blown softly into
her hair. When Cara had looked into his big
dark brown eyes she'd known that here was
a new friend she could trust.

"Hey, babe," she'd whispered as she ran a
hand along his beautiful silky neck.

Vicki, who was standing next to Cara,
had smiled as she made friends with Taffy.

"Good choice. Taffy's the kindest and sturdiest pony in my yard," she'd said.

Cara had giggled as cheeky Taffy nudged her gently in the tummy. "That's his way of telling you he wants a treat," Vicki had explained.

Putting a mint on the flat of her palm, she'd held out her hand to Taffy, who lifted his lips and carefully took the mint between his front teeth. Cara had laughed as he crunched it loudly. Then Vicki put a mint on Cara's palm.

"You hold one out to him now," she'd said.

Cara's big blue eyes had opened wide.

"He won't hurt you, honestly," Vicki had told her.

Cara had nervously held out her hand and Taffy had helped himself to a second mint, tickling Cara's palm as he took it.

"You're gorgeous," she'd said with a giggle.

After that, Cara rode Taffy every Saturday. But because she loved him so much she visited him all the other days as well, even in the winter after school, when it was horrible and wet. Seeing how dedicated she was, Vicki had given Cara jobs to do for Taffy: grooming him, cleaning his tack, mucking out his stable, mixing his feeds and filling his hay-net. Cara loved doing all these jobs, but most of all she just loved being close to Taffy.

Eventually Vicki had made Cara a yard girl. This meant she was in charge of one pony – Taffy – but had to help out generally around the stables too. In return, Vicki gave her a free riding lesson every Saturday. Cara was now learning to jump on Taffy, and Vicki said that she was making good progress.

Through Taffy, Cara had got to know the other yard girls. Pretty Jess with her long brown hair and twinkling green eyes, who looked after Rose; clever Amber, who was in charge of Stella; Sam, the joker of the group, who looked after Beanz; and tough Mel, who was a brilliant show-jumper already and looked after Candy.

Cara had been shy with the girls to start with, but they were all so friendly it hadn't taken her long to become one of their gang. After all, they all had one massive thing in common: they were pony mad!

Cara and her new friends also totally hero-worshipped Vicki, who ran a good yard and kept her horses and ponies in great condition. She was really pretty, with thick dark hair, tanned skin and big silver-grey eyes. Vicki was living proof that you could be glam and still be a brilliant horsewoman!

There were other girls at the stables but they owned their ponies, which they kept at livery. Cara and her friends got on really well with one of the livery girls: Darcy was good fun to hang around with. She had a long dark plait that dangled down her back and ended just below her bottom. Her pony, Duke, was a dark bay show-jumper with a stable full of rosettes.

Darcy wasn't like the other snooty livery girls. She went to a posh school like they did and her parents weren't short of cash but she was different. Darcy enjoyed having a laugh with the yard girls, and when she had time, she always mucked out Duke's stable, mixed his feeds and filled his hay-net.

Henrietta Reece-Thomas and Camilla Worthington couldn't have been more different though. They were also livery girls, but neither of them would ever sink so low as to muck out a pony's stable or mix a feed! Their parents paid Vicki to do that and the yard girls had a weekly livery rota, which meant that two of them were responsible for feeding, grooming and mucking out the livery ponies. Cara was scared stiff of Henrietta and Camilla and dreaded her weeks on the rota. Luckily she was always on livery duty with Mel who wasn't frightened of anybody, not even moody Henrietta.

So thanks to Taffy and all her friends at Vicki's stables, Cara had got over many of her fears, and here she was now, packing her bag for her first pony club weekend. There was no way she could have done that a year ago.

Cara's daydreaming was interrupted by
her mum calling from downstairs, "Are you
all right, love?"

Cara jumped off the bed and ran to her
open bedroom door. "I can't do up my
rucksack," she called back.

Cara's mum came hurrying upstairs,
and between them they managed to close
the rucksack after repacking it a couple
of times.

"There you are, all ready to go," said her mum.

Cara looked at her smiling face and started to nibble her nails, something she did when she was nervous.

Mum smiled knowingly. "What is it, sweetie? Come on, spit it out."

So Cara blurted out what was worrying her. "I want to go to the pony club weekend, I really do," she cried. "But we haven't been apart since Dad died and I'll feel weird going away without you."

"Come here," said her mum, and she sat down on the bed beside Cara and gave her a hug.

Cara sniffed in the warm smell of her mum's hair and perfume. "I love you, Mum," she muttered tearfully.

Her mum squeezed her even harder. "And I love you too, gorgeous, but I'm glad you're going away. You need to get out there and have some fun. You'll have a brilliant time and Taffy will too – and don't forget I'm coming to watch you at the gymkhana tomorrow afternoon," she said.

Cara smiled and kissed her mum on both cheeks. "Well, if you're sure. I promise I won't let you down," she said.

"That's my girl!"

A ring on the doorbell made them both jump.

"That'll be Mel," said Cara.

As Mum ran downstairs to open the front door, Cara picked up her rucksack, kissed the photograph of her dad, then legged it out of the room.

Mel was waiting in the hall with a big grin on her face. Cara thought Mel was really pretty. She had a mass of curly black hair, big dark eyes, soft brown skin and a cute little turned-up nose.

"Ready to go? Got everything?" Mel asked.

Cara nodded. "I've even packed a hot-water bottle," she laughed. "It might get cold camping out in that barn."

"Did you remember stuff for the midnight feast?" Mel asked her.

Cara put a hand to her mouth. "No way! I can't believe I nearly forgot!"

As she went into the kitchen to pick up the bag of sweets and biscuits, her mum turned to Mel. "It's really kind of your dad to give Cara a lift," she said. "Thanks a lot."

Mel grinned. "No worries. But if she's got as much stuff as me, we're gonna need a forklift truck to unload the car!" she said with a laugh.

Chapter 2

It was the August bank holiday weekend
so the roads were busy with holidaymakers
getting the last of the summer sun. As Mel's
dad drove them to Vicki's yard, the girls
chatted excitedly. Vicki had told them that
there were five groups coming to the pony
club weekend and competing in the games.
Each group had six people in it and had
been given a different colour. Cara, Mel
and their friends were in the pink group.
Henrietta, Camilla and four other girls
from Henrietta's posh school were in the
purple group. The three other groups, made
up of boys and girls from riding schools

nearby, were red, blue and green.

Mel gave a long whistle. "Vicki's yard's gonna be packed with thirty riders charging around," she said.

Keeping his eyes on the busy road, Mel's dad, who was a policeman, gave a deep chuckle. "I hope there'll be enough toilets for you all," he teased.

Mel sighed. "Trust you to think of something like that, Dad," she said.

Behind Mel's dad's back, Cara gave her friend a nudge. "But he's right though – no way will there be enough loos for us all," she whispered.

Mel giggled. "We'll have to go behind hedges or dig a hole or something!" she said.

The thought of all thirty of them squatting behind a hedge made Cara burst out laughing. "You're an idiot, Mel!" she said, and chuckled all the way to the yard.

They couldn't get up the driveway because of all the horseboxes parked there so Mel's dad dropped them off at the gate.

Caution
Horses!
Reduce
Speed

"Have fun and be good," he called as he drove off.

Mel grinned. "We will, Dad," she replied.

Both girls lifted their heavy rucksacks onto their backs and Mel picked up a suitcase she'd brought too.

"What you got in there?" Cara asked as they struggled up the drive.

Mel shrugged. "I couldn't make my mind up what to wear so I just dumped all my clothes in the case!" she laughed.

They found Jess, Amber, Darcy and Sam in the empty tack room.

"Quick, come in and shut the door," said Jess as they stumbled in with their heavy bags.

Mel slammed the door shut and Sam groaned as she tried to lift Mel's suitcase. "Phew! You got bricks in there?" she asked.

Amber pointed to the piece of card that was pinned up on the notice board. "Look at this," she told them.

Vicki had stuck up the timetable for the weekend, and the six of them got in each other's way as they all tried to look at it at the same time. Sunday was the big gymkhana day, when all five teams would be competing, but today looked pretty busy too. Jess read out loud from the board.

"Ten o'clock, arrive, and groom and tack up your ponies. Eleven o'clock, jumping class in the outdoor school. Twelve o'clock, lunch. Two o'clock, practise gymkhana team-games. Four o'clock, turn ponies out into the meadow for the night. Five o'clock, campfire supper. Six o'clock, prepare tack. Seven o'clock, cocoa and pony quiz competition. Nine o'clock, lights out."

When Jess stopped reading, the girls reacted in their very different ways.

"Wow! This is going to be wicked!" Mel said excitedly.

Jess wound a strand of her thick brown hair round her fingers, thinking hard. "The ponies are going to get so over-excited when they're surrounded by a load of new ponies they've never seen before," she said.

And Sam, who was hyper all the time, just spun round in a circle. "Beanz is gonna love making friends with them all!" she giggled.

Darcy, organized as usual, checked out where they were sleeping. "Says here we're in the oat barn so we should dump our stuff over there now, I reckon," she said.

But Cara looked worried. All she could think about was the jumping class at eleven o'clock. "Is it compulsory?" she asked nervously.

The other girls knew how timid Cara could be when faced with new things and people, so they all smiled at her.

"Nothing's compulsory but it would be good practice, Car," Amber replied.

Cara nibbled her fingernails. "But I'm not used to jumping in front of strangers," she blurted out. "I'm no way good enough yet!"

Sam giggled. "Don't worry, Car. Taffy will be on automatic pilot – he'll do all the hard work for you."

Mel gave Cara a gentle pat on the back. "Give it a go and see how you feel," she suggested.

Cara smiled weakly, then nodded her head. "Taffy would never forgive me if I didn't!" she said.

They carried their stuff over to the barn, which was beside the meadow where the ponies were grazing. The girls stopped to check they were OK.

As soon as he saw Cara, Taffy came cantering over and nuzzled up against her. Cara patted him gently. "Hello, lovely boy. Are you ready for this weekend? I hope you're not as nervous as me."

Taffy neighed loudly and shook his silky golden head. The others all laughed.

"See, Taffy's totally laid back!" said Mel.

Suddenly Sam let out a loud shout. "Oh, no! Look at Beanz!"

They all turned to see the skewbald
rolling in a muddy patch by the stream.
Sam shook her spiky ginger hair and
smiled so widely all the freckles on her nose
wrinkled up.

"Great! Now I'll have to spend ages
scraping mud off him!" she said with a
laugh. "Typical!"

The girls left the ponies and wandered over to the barn. The ground floor contained all the feed sacks and the upper floor was where the hay and straw were kept. The girls pushed together a double row of straw bales to make their beds and put their sleeping bags and pillows on top. All of them had different patterned pony sleeping bags. Mel had show-jumpers on hers, Amber's had pony heads, Sam had funny bucking cartoon ponies on hers, Darcy's had galloping ponies, Jess's had horseshoes and Cara's sleeping bag was decorated with a big picture of Taffy, which her mum had got printed on the cover as a birthday present.

As they were busy unpacking, a van drove past the barn. Jess, who was nearest the window, looked out and gave a shout.

"You are so not gonna believe who's just driven by in a mobile-home thing," she said.

All the girls ran to the window to have a look themselves. They couldn't believe their eyes when they saw the shiny white mobile home pull up in the camping field and Henrietta Reece-Thomas jump out. She was followed by five other girls, including Camilla Worthington. As grumpy Mr Reece-Thomas unhitched the mobile home from his four-wheel drive, Cara and the others realized that snooty Henrietta and her friends were no way roughing it like the rest of them.

"Typical! They're staying in luxury accommodation while the rest of us slum it!" gasped Jess.

"I bet they've got a microwave in there," said Amber.

"And a fridge and a shower," Darcy added.

Mel giggled. "There's bound to be a toilet in there too. No crouching behind hedges for Miss Snooty Knickers!" she said.

Sam pulled a funny face and put on a posh voice. "Dah-ling, Daddy wouldn't want me to mix with the low life!" she mimicked.

"I wouldn't want to be sleeping next to Henrietta anyway," Cara said.

"You wouldn't get any sleep because she'd be bossing you about all night," Darcy giggled.

Mel couldn't take her eyes off the mobile home. "I've got to check it out," she said.

Jess looked at the pink pony clock she'd put beside her hay-bale bed. "Not now, Mel, it's nearly ten — we'd better get a move on," she said.

In the meadow the ponies were wild with excitement. The sight of so many strange ponies arriving on foot and in rumbling horseboxes had sent them well over the top. Steady Rose and gentle Stella weren't too hard for Jess and Amber to catch, and Taffy just trotted up to Cara like always, expecting a mint and a kiss! But Beanz, Candy and Duke were having a great time and didn't want to leave! Every time Sam got near Beanz he shied then galloped away. Poor Sam ran after him until she couldn't run any more. Stubborn Candy just cantered round the field so Mel didn't stand a chance of catching her, and Duke was being just as awkward. In the end the girls had to work

together to catch the three ponies, who
were sweating in the heat. Holding a length
of rope behind their backs, they cornered
them at the top of the field so it was easy to
throw a headcollar around their necks and
clip a lead rope to it. By the end of it they
were sweating almost as much as the ponies.

"I'm shattered before we've even started!" gasped Sam.

Mel was so hot she stuck her head in a bucket of water, wetting her dark curls.

The girls tied up their ponies, who stamped and fidgeted at the flies buzzing around their eyes as they were groomed. Just as they were all tacked up, Henrietta came stomping by.

"Why is President still in his box?" she snapped.

Mel and Cara, who were on livery rota that week, looked at each other in confusion.

President was Henrietta's stunning spotty grey Appaloosa. He'd been shipped over from the States by Henrietta's wealthy

parents as a surprise present for her. But
Cara always felt sorry for him. Henrietta
never cuddled him, but Cara knew that he
was a really sweet pony who wanted lots of
love.

"You're supposed to sort out your own
ponies this weekend," Mel said quickly.

Henrietta tossed her silky blonde hair,
which was cut in a very expensive bob. "My
father doesn't pay good money for me to do
the dirty work around here," she said coldly.

Cara blushed with embarrassment. All
she needed was for Henrietta to have a go
at her just before the dreaded showjumping
lesson.

Luckily Vicki arrived on the scene. "You
should be heading for the outdoor school by
now," she said to Henrietta, who scowled
crossly.

"Camilla and I are waiting for somebody
to tack up our ponies," she replied.

Vicki shook her head. "The idea of pony club camp is that we all look after our *own* ponies. That means we do everything for them. I thought I'd made that very clear."

Henrietta gave Cara a dirty look. "Thanks for nothing," she snapped, and then she stomped off to break the bad news to Camilla.

The jumping lesson lasted until lunch time. All thirty riders were trying to get round the challenging course of gates, parallels, tyres and brightly coloured barrels with cross bars that Vicki had set up. Vicki wasn't the only adult around. Susie, who helped her in the stables, was there and so were quite a few teachers from the other schools, who'd come along to give advice and moral support to their groups.

Chewing on her fingernails again, Cara watched the different groups tackle the course. "Some of them are brilliant," she gasped.

Sam pointed to one of Henrietta's snooty friends: her little Arab was charging straight at a fence but obviously had no intention of jumping it. "And some of them are really rubbish," she said.

To prove her point, the pony bolted out of the ring with the inexperienced rider gripping onto his mane.

"Honestly, Car, you've got absolutely nothing to worry about."

★

The pink group were the last but one to go, and when the moment came, they all did really well. Beanz stopped shying and showing off and really knuckled down to the course. Sam reined him in with all her strength and he cleared every jump. Candy was as graceful as ever and it was obvious to everyone that Mel was definitely the best show-jumper there. Rose did a perfect round; Stella did well too, though she did try to take the parallel bar too quickly and nearly knocked off the pole, and Duke, under Darcy's careful guidance, got a clap from the crowd for his speed and confidence.

Finally it was Cara's turn. Seeing her white face as she entered the ring, Vicki patted her arm and said softly, "Don't worry, babe. Just trust Taffy and you'll be fine."

Cara nodded and smiled weakly but Taffy wasn't bothered at all. He tossed his

pretty head
and trotted
into the ring
with his long
blond tail
swooping out
like a golden
flag. As Cara
fumbled with
her reins and
awkwardly
adjusted her
seat, Taffy

took control. Ignoring his rider's nerves, he
approached every jump on the right leg,
popped over the lot and finished with an
excellent clear round. As Cara galloped out
of the ring, she laughed with a mixture of
joy, pride and relief. She reined him in and
quickly dismounted to bury her face in his
sweet-smelling mane.

"You're the best little pony in the world!" she told him.

As Taffy nudged her for a mint treat, Cara gave him a kiss on both his ears, then tickled his velvety soft nose!

Chapter 3

The day stayed hot so everybody took
their lunch outside. The girls lay in the
meadow where the tents were pitched and
watched the ponies in the fields getting
to know each other. Rose was nuzzling a
pretty dark Dale pony; Stella was making
friends with a lively Exmoor; Beanz was
chasing after a Welsh Mountain mare and
Candy was nibbling a grey Fell pony who
looked all set to give her a kick!

The girls laughed at the ponies as
they unpacked their picnics and did their
usual swapping of sandwiches, crisps
and biscuits.

Darcy spotted a girl from her school in
one of the other groups, and Mel and Amber
waved to a boy who was in their class.

"Everyone's dead friendly here," said Jess.

Sam pulled a funny face. "Some people
aren't." Her eyes rolled sideways towards
Henrietta's posh mobile home. She, Camilla

and their friends were sitting outside it
round a table eating pasta from proper
plates with silver cutlery!

"Who do they think they are?" giggled
Amber.

Mel suddenly got to her feet and winked
at Cara. "Want to go for a walk?" she asked.

Cara was surprised by Mel's question but she didn't like to say no so she stood up too and they set off.

"Where are we going?" Cara asked.

Mel giggled and leaned close to whisper in Cara's ear. "For a look round the little princesses' home!" she said.

Cara stopped. "No way, Mel!" she squeaked nervously. "Henrietta's sitting right outside."

Mel took hold of her arm and pulled her along. "I'm only talking about looking through the windows round the back," she said quickly. "Chill out. Henrietta'll never know."

They crept round to the back of the mobile home and stared through the window into the lounge.

"Wow! It's posher than our lounge at home!" gasped Cara.

The room had a soft cream carpet, a

leather three-piece suite, an oval-shaped
glass coffee table with a crystal vase of red
roses on it, a massive flat screen TV and a
flashy stereo system.

Mel gave Cara a dig in the ribs with
her elbow. "Let's go round the side," she
whispered.

They couldn't believe their eyes when
they saw the bathroom through a gap
in the blinds.

"It's like
something out
of a magazine!"
giggled Cara.

There was a
walk-in shower in
a glass cubicle that
looked big enough
for two people. The
shower head was

as big as a frying pan and the circular bath
had gold taps and a Jacuzzi!

"Imagine lying in a Jacuzzi full of bubbles
after riding and working at the stables all
day," said Mel in a dreamy voice.

It was while they were staring open-
mouthed through the kitchen window that
Henrietta caught them. They'd spotted the
microwave, dishwasher, washing machine
and dryer and were busy checking out the
juicer when she came up behind them.

"Would you like a guided tour?" she snapped.

Cara was lost for words but Mel didn't seem bothered at all. "We were just passing," she blagged.

Henrietta's eyes were ice-cold. "I don't suppose you're used to luxurious living," she said with a sneer.

Cara felt Mel stiffen with anger. She began to feel nervous – was Mel going to pick a fight? They shouldn't have been there spying!

Mel took a deep breath. "Not all of us are well off, no," she said, "but being spoiled's not something to be proud of," and she stalked off.

As Cara dashed after her, Henrietta called out to them, "If I catch you trespassing again, I'll have you reported."

Cara's heart was pounding but Mel turned round coolly and said, "Sure. My dad's a policeman. I'll get you his number if you want."

Cara and Mel found their friends lying on the soft warm grass making daisy chains. They jumped up when they saw the girls running towards them.

"You were a long time," said Jess.

Mel laughed as she threw herself down on the grass. "We went for a look round Henrietta's mobile home," she explained.

Cara sat down beside her and nodded sheepishly.

Sam arranged her daisy chain garland on Cara's long blonde hair. "So, come on. What's it like?" she asked.

"It's well posh. They've got a walk-in shower, Jacuzzi, hi-fi, massive TV — looks like a shop!" Cara said, running out of breath.

"It's pretty cool," agreed Mel, sounding a little bit jealous.

Amber smiled. "Yeah. Henrietta's parents are obviously loaded but have you ever seen her look happy?" she asked.

Mel shook her head. "She's always in a mood," she said.

Sam giggled. "You're right, Amber, loads of money doesn't make you happy — it just makes you rich!" she joked.

Cara lay back and stared up at the blue sky, which was dotted with little puffy

clouds. She sighed happily. "Who needs
dosh when you can do this?" she said. "I
was well nervous about coming but I'm glad
Mum persuaded me."

Her perfect moment was suddenly ruined
by a hot wet slurp on her cheek! "Ahhh!"
cried Cara, sitting bolt upright. She quickly
looked round and saw where the slurp had
come from. The puppies, Treasure and
Hunt, were scampering around her bare
feet. Cara stretched forward and scooped
them up into her arms.

"Cheeky monkeys!" she giggled.

The puppies loved all the girls but they were especially devoted to Cara and Mel, who had rescued them from drowning in a freezing-cold millpond.

As the puppies snuggled up between the girls, stuffing their faces with leftover crusts and scraps of crisps, the girls ran down the list of gymkhana games. Seeing the list made Cara start to feel nervous again.

"I can't do the relay race," she said. "I'm not fast enough."

Darcy gave her a comforting pat on the arm. "Don't worry, babe. Just do the games you feel confident about," she suggested.

Amber looked up. "Best turned-out pony is definitely for you though, Car," she said.

"What do I have to do?" Cara asked.

Amber grinned. "A lot of grooming to make sure that you and Taffy are the smartest pony and rider here."

"I'd enjoy that," Cara said with a smile.

All the other girls really fancied the relay race.

"We have to go fast and pass a baton like in a normal relay race," Jess explained. "But there's only space for four riders on the team."

For a minute nobody wanted to be the one to volunteer not to race and they all just looked at each other.

Finally Amber said, "I suppose I'm the slowest out of us since I broke my arm. I don't mind really – I'll do the canter bit of the walk, trot and canter race so I get a bit of speedy riding this weekend!"

Jess gave her best friend's hand a quick squeeze. "Thanks, babe," she said.

"Yeah, thanks, Amber," Mel said. "I think I'd have trouble not going fast on Candy."

"There'll be two of us cheering you on

now, so you'll definitely win," said Cara grinning.

Darcy looked thoughtful. "We'll have to be really careful though, even if we are trying to go quickly, cos otherwise we won't be able to pass the baton," she pointed out.

Sam burst out laughing. "I can see I'm going to have to do a lot of practice baton-passing on Beanz this afternoon!"

Cara wanted to do the sack race and the potato race, Mel was definitely going in for the showjumping competition, and Jess suggested they all did the walk, trot and canter race. Putting them into two teams, she suggested, "How about me, Amber and Darcy; then Mel, Sam and Cara."

Mel nudged Cara and winked at her. "Before you start panicking, you can do the walking, Sam can do the trotting and I'll finish off with a fantastic canter!" she said with a laugh.

Before the practice session for the games started, Mel and Cara carried the naughty puppies back to Vicki's pretty cottage, which was in the yard next to the main driveway. Giving each of the pups a kiss on the nose, the girls tucked them into their basket then ran back to the field to catch their ponies. On their way they passed President and Cleopatra, who were in their stables. Cara had a quick look inside and was annoyed to see President pacing his stable with his saddle still on.

"You'd think Henrietta could at least have loosened his girth before she sat down to have her stupid posh dinner," she fumed.

Mel frowned. "Putting President first would be too much like hard work for Henrietta," she said.

They were in a hurry, but Cara couldn't resist opening President's stable door. "Hello, sweetheart," she said.

The beautiful Appaloosa whinnied softly then moved over to Cara, who stroked his spotty coat.

"Who's a beautiful boy?" she said.

President pressed his soft nose into her chest and blew heavily against her. Cara smiled as she tickled his ears and carried on chatting to him.

"Do you want a cuddle, babe?" she asked.

Their quiet moment was interrupted by the sound of Henrietta's harsh voice.

"You two seem determined to be in my face all day!" she said angrily.

Cara jumped guiltily away from President. "Er, I was just giving him a cuddle," she spluttered.

"He's my pony so you can leave that to me. Now get out of my sight before I really lose my temper!" Henrietta barked.

Mel squared up to her. "Well, if he's your pony, shouldn't you have sorted him out before you sat down to your fancy lunch?"

"What are you talking about?" said Henrietta. "He's in his stable, I've given him a bucket of water—"

"And left his saddle on," Mel pointed out.

"Oh, mind your own business!"

"The welfare of the ponies *is* our business," said Mel, and she and Cara hurried away, leaving Henrietta scowling.

"The idea of Henrietta looking after anything makes me laugh," said Mel crossly.

55

"Yeah, me too." Cara remembered how Henrietta had wanted to leave Treasure and Hunt to drown. "She doesn't care about ponies any more than she cares about puppies."

Chapter 4

At two o'clock the five teams practised
gymkhana games in the two largest fields:
one was laid out with jumps while the other
was set up for the racing games. The riding
teachers kept an eye on their groups, giving
them tips and timing them. Cara loved the
sack race, which she did with Amber and
Sam. Taffy might have won the race if
naughty Beanz hadn't eaten all the potatoes!

Sitting astride Taffy, Cara watched her
friends line up for the start of the relay race,
but she was shocked when she overheard
Henrietta speaking to her posh friends.

"We'll easily beat the pink team – their

ponies are a bunch of clapped-out old nags!"

"Did you hear that?" Cara asked Amber.

"Yeah," said Amber. "Silly cow. How dare she? I really hope we win. And she'd better not let Vicki hear her saying things like that about the ponies!"

Fortunately for Henrietta, Vicki didn't hear her nasty comments; otherwise she'd have been in big trouble. Vicki was too busy explaining the rules of the relay race.

"Slow down as you approach your teammate so that you can pass the baton without dropping it. If you do drop it, dismount and pick it up then pass it on. Control is what counts in this race," she told them.

Cara watched, open-mouthed with excitement, as Mel set off on Candy against Henrietta on President. They both went like the wind, but when it came to passing the baton, Henrietta completely ignored Vicki's good advice. She thundered up the track towards Camilla and hurled the baton at her.

Mel charged up the track too, but she was controlling Candy, neatly turning her in order to place the baton in Jess's open hand.

Camilla tried to catch the baton but missed it and it fell to the floor. As she quickly dismounted to pick it up, Henrietta bawled at her, "You stupid girl!"

Camilla scowled but didn't hang about to argue. Mounting up, she galloped down the line after Jess, who was already on her way back up.

Vicki glanced at Henrietta, who was red in the face. "I told you to control your pony as you made your approach to pass the baton," she said.

"I *did* control him. Can I help it if Camilla dropped it?" she snapped.

"Only because you threw it at her," Vicki pointed out.

Before Henrietta could make any reply, Vicki turned away to watch Sam come galloping up to pass the baton neatly to Darcy, who was the last rider to go in their group. She gave Duke his head and he easily overtook the fourth rider in Henrietta's team, bringing glory to the pink team. All six girls, Cara and Amber included, screamed their heads off as Darcy cleared the finishing line.

Vicki smiled at their excited, smiling faces.
"Well done!" she said.

Sensing their mood, the
over-excited ponies tossed
their heads and pawed
the ground
impatiently.

Vicki patted
frisky Candy.
"I think you'd
better take
them for a nice
gentle stroll to
calm them down,"
she said.

They took her good advice and walked
off on their ponies, but Amber couldn't resist
saying something to Henrietta.

As she passed the snooty girls, she stared
at them. "Not bad for a bunch of useless old
nags, eh?" Amber said.

After the ponies had calmed down, the girls untacked them then gave them a good grooming before turning them out into the meadow for the night. In a giggly mood, the girls ran into the barn, where they'd left plastic bags containing their tea.

"I've never cooked sausage and beans over a campfire," said Cara excitedly.

Sam tossed a tin of beans up in the air and grinned. "I hope Beanz doesn't hear you say that – he might take it personally," she joked.

Mel set up a little gas fire, which her older brothers had shown her how to use. Sitting in the camping field, which was still warm and sunny, they found a flat patch to put their little cooker on, then started to prepare their tea. The smell of sizzling sausages and bubbling beans made their mouths water. Cara buttered thick slices of crusty bread as Darcy set the table, which was a blanket thrown down on the grass.

"I'm starving," Cara said.

Darcy looked up at her and grinned. "Don't tell me you could eat a horse!" she teased.

Cara giggled and shook her head. "No, but I could eat a million sausages!"

The hot sausages, which they ate stuffed inside the fresh bread and smothered in

beans, were delicious. For pudding they
shared out Jess's bag of cherries, Amber's
home-made cake, Sam's little pots of jelly,
Darcy's biscuits, Mel's oranges and Cara's
fruit yoghurts.

Jess rubbed her belly and groaned. "Oh,
I'm stuffed!"

Amber rolled onto her front and started to
make another daisy chain. "It's the fresh air
that's made us so hungry," she said.

Sam tried juggling with her cherries and ended up dropping them all. "And chasing after naughty ponies who didn't want to be caught," she added.

Cara grinned as she saw Henrietta and her friends serving themselves cold quiche and salad from plastic coolers. "Look at them! But I bet their posh tea isn't half as good as ours!" she said.

After washing up in the stream, where they splashed each other more than their cups and plates, the girls raced over to the tack room to polish their ponies' tack ready for the next day. Hearing their giggles, Treasure and Hunt came scampering across the yard and started to nibble at the bridles that were dangling over the edge of the table.

"No, no, no!" cried Amber.

Darcy bent down to pick up the naughty

pups, who immediately started to chew on her long brown plait. She held them out to Cara.

"Go to Auntie Cara," she said with a laugh.

For the first time ever Cara shook her head. "I can't play with them now – I've got to clean Taffy's tack,"  she explained. "I really want him to look good for the best-groomed pony competition tomorrow."

So Mel played with Treasure and Hunt, who were having fun ripping an old woollen blanket to bits, and Cara polished Taffy's bridle and bit until they shone. Then she started on his saddle. The best turned-out pony event was her one chance to win a prize. She might not be a brave jumper or a brilliant horsewoman but she could certainly clean tack better than anybody else in the yard!

The girls got so carried away cleaning their tack they forgot the time until Jess looked at her watch. "It's nearly seven o'clock. We don't want to be late for Vicki's pony club quiz," she said.

Cara shook her head and carried on polishing her stirrups. "I'm not coming until I've finished these," she said firmly.

Sam laughed as she examined her reflection in the already spotlessly clean stirrups. "If you buff them up any more you'll blind the judges!" she teased.

Mel gave Cara a gentle poke in the ribs with her finger. "Come on, Car, you'll rub a hole in that saddle if you polish it any more," she said.

"Just five minutes," Cara promised. "I'll catch you up."

Chapter 5

When she'd finished cleaning Taffy's tack, Cara found the others waiting for the quiz to begin. It was being held in the camping field. Vicki had worked really hard on the quiz: first she handed round ten questions she'd written to all five teams. The team that got the fewest right would be out at the end of the first round. Then Vicki would hand out another ten questions. Again, the team that came last was out. After three rounds, Cara's pink team and Henrietta's purple team, who had been at loggerheads all day, made it through to the final.

Henrietta sneered as she looked across at the pink team. "They're so thick they don't stand a chance against us," she said to her snooty friends.

Vicki handed each team a set of five final questions. "The first team to answer all the questions correctly is the winner," she said.

In a low voice Jess quickly read out the first question: "Why shouldn't you let your pony eat as much grass as he likes in the spring?" she said.

Amber instantly knew the answer. "Because he might get laminitis," she hissed into Jess's ear.

As Jess scribbled down the answer, Cara saw Camilla sneakily making a call. She couldn't believe it when she whispered into her mobile phone. After a pause she muttered something to Henrietta, who wrote down an answer on the question sheet.

Cara tapped Darcy on the arm. "The purple team are cheating!" she spluttered in shock.

Darcy and the others quickly looked over at Henrietta's team and saw Camilla hide the mobile phone behind her back. "Did you get good reception?" Mel yelled at the top of her voice.

All the competitors looked up as Vicki called out, "If I find anybody cheating in any way, their team will be immediately disqualified."

Camilla blushed, but Henrietta tossed her smartly bobbed blonde hair. "The pink team have been using a mobile phone," she lied.

As Cara and her friends
gasped in amazement, Vicki
quickly walked over to them with
a frown on her pretty suntanned
face. "Have any of you got a
mobile phone?" she snapped.

Everyone except Darcy shook their heads. "I've got one but it's switched off," Darcy told her.

And at that moment Camilla's ring tone sounded with a loud squeaky jingle. Vicki turned and held out her hand. "I'll have that," she said crossly.

As she walked away with Camilla's pink phone, Cara's team frantically tried to make up for lost time. Amber read out the next question. "How many faults do you get for a refusal in a showjumping competition?"

Mel grabbed the pencil and wrote down the answer: three faults. As she wrote, Jess read out the next question. "Name three obstacles you would find on a cross-country jumping course."

Cara looked blank but Mel let out an excited whoop, which made her friends hiss at her in case she gave away the answer.

As Mel scribbled down the answer, Cara

read what she'd written: tree trunks, ditches and banks. "Well done," she whispered in her friend's ear.

Sam read out the fourth question: "What's a frog?"

It was Darcy's turn to grab the pencil and write down the answer: the soft squishy shock absorber in the middle of a pony's sole.

After a brilliant start they all got stuck on the fifth and final question, which was: What do you call a young male horse up to the age of three years old? They would have lost the quiz altogether if Cara hadn't suddenly remembered the word. Snatching the pencil, she speedily wrote down the answer: a colt.

As Amber, Mel, Sam and Darcy slapped Cara on the back, Jess ran across to Vicki and handed over their finished question sheet. She was followed closely by Henrietta, who dashed up with her team's sheet. Cara held her breath as Vicki read their answers.

"They're both correct but the pink team finished first so they're the winners!" she said.

As Jess and her friends skipped around, clapping and cheering, Henrietta's face looked like thunder! She stomped back to her team and complained loudly, "They cheated of course!"

Chapter 6

Clutching their prize of a box of chocolates, the pink team hurried back to the barn, which they lit by hanging their torches from the rafters. It looked so snug and cosy, with their colourful sleeping bags laid out ready for them on the hay bales. The girls washed their hands and faces under the tap they used to fill up the ponies' water buckets. The shock of the cold water made Cara jump.

"It's freezing!" she cried.

Sam sprayed water up in the air, wetting their pyjamas as she did so. "Good for your skin!" she joked.

They cleaned their teeth, which was a bit of a waste of time because as soon as they got back into the barn they started scoffing their midnight feast! To Cara's surprise she found she was too tired to eat more than four chocolates – the excitement of the day plus all the exercise and fresh air had finally got to her and she felt her eyelids start to droop. Yawning her head off, she snuggled down into her soft warm sleeping bag.

"Ahhh, this is gorgeous!" she said.

Then she felt a sharp nibbling at her feet. Thinking it was rats, Cara jumped out of her sleeping bag. "Help!" she yelled.

Mel was at her side in a flash. As they shook out the sleeping bag between them, they discovered that it wasn't rats that had bitten Cara's toes – it was the puppies!

"They must have sneaked in here while we were doing the quiz," said Amber.

Looking really cute, Treasure and Hunt

rolled over onto their backs and squeaked sleepily. Cara picked them up and tucked them back inside the sleeping bag, then snuggled down beside them.

Darcy reached out for her mobile, which was on a nearby hay bale. "I'd better phone Vicki and tell her the pups are safe here with us," she said with a smile.

As owls hooted outside and the puppies slept peacefully beside her, Cara sighed happily. She couldn't believe she'd been scared of coming away – this was pure bliss!

She was just getting really comfortable when Sam said, "Um, guys . . . did you just hear something?"

"No," said Mel sleepily. "And shut up, will you? I was just about to drop off."

"Sorry," Sam whispered. "It's just sometimes I freak myself out when I'm in the barn on my own, or it's a bit dark."

"Why?" asked Jess. "Stuff like that doesn't normally bother you."

"I know," Sam answered in a low voice. "But Vicki told me this story about headless riders on phantom white horses galloping through the countryside," she said in a scary voice.

With only one torch left on to light the room, Cara couldn't see her friends' faces properly but she could hear them all breathing.

"*No!*" they all whispered.

Cara's skin began to crawl as Sam began her ghost story.

"They were a brotherhood of monks who were killed when soldiers rode through their abbey, smashing the statues and burning things."

Cara started to imagine the horrible scene of the burning abbey and the screaming monks. She shivered with fear as Sam continued.

"The brotherhood were imprisoned by the heartless soldiers, who locked them up in dark dungeons crawling with rats," Sam said in a hushed voice.

Cara's blonde hair felt like it was going to stand on end as she heard a scary tip-tapping noise at the window. "Stop making those weird noises, Sam, you're scaring me to death," she said in a shaky voice.

Sam was so into her story she took no

notice of Cara, who was now sitting on her hay-bale bed with her sleeping bag pulled up to her chin.

"One by one the soldiers executed the poor monks, who had never harmed a soul. They chopped off their heads and buried them in unhallowed ground," Sam whispered.

By this time the other girls had heard the tip-tapping at the window, which was followed by a loud, eerie howl. Darcy was trying to be sensible. "It's only an owl," she reassured them.

Mel ran over to Cara's hay-bale bed and cuddled up beside her. "Give it a rest, Sam!" she said tensely.

But there was no stopping Sam when she was into a story. "The dead monks knew no peace — they rose headless from their shallow graves and haunted the soldiers who had destroyed their abbey. They hounded

them down one by one until they too were
all dead."

As Sam finished the dreadful story,
something flew up at the barn window.
Out of the corner of her eye Cara saw a
white, floaty shape. "Argh!" she screamed
in terror.

The other girls, who by now were also
sitting bolt upright, glanced at Sam.

"Are you playing tricks on us?" Jess asked.

Sam switched on her torch and looked at her friends' scared faces. "Cross my heart and hope to die I haven't set anything up," she said.

Her flashing torch lit up the huge barn with tall, dark, spooky shadows. A shiver ran down Cara's spine like ice. "Oooh, I'm so scared!" she said in a trembling voice.

As the high-pitched howling noises continued outside, brave Mel grabbed her torch and ran to the window.

"Be careful!" Darcy called out.

Mel pressed her face against the window and shone the torch out across the yard. "Argh!" she screamed suddenly.

Her scream shocked the other girls, and they ran to her side. Cara clutched nervously onto the back of Amber's pyjamas as they stood together and stared out the window. Then they saw what had frightened Mel. There were howling ghostly shapes running around the yard!

Cara couldn't look any more and ran back to her bed, burrowing down into her sleeping bag so she couldn't see anything.

"Is it the headless monks coming to get us?" she asked, her eyes starting to fill with tears under the covers.

Mel pulled herself together and had a good look at the spooky figures. "Wait a minute . . ." she said. "Why has one of the ghosts got stupid purple slippers on?" She flung open the window and chucked an empty Coke can down into the yard. It landed with a loud clang. The ghost wearing the slippers screamed in surprise. The ghost next to her pulled the white sheet off her head and said, "Stop making so much noise, Sophie, you idiot. You'll spoil all the fun."

The girls would have recognized that snappy voice anywhere. It was Henrietta, and the other ghosts were her friends covered in white sheets!

Sam stuck her
head out of the
window next
to Mel. "You
total losers!" she
shouted. "Haven't
you got anything
better to do?"

Hearing Sam's shouts, Cara stuck her
head back out of her sleeping bag. But
before she could say anything, Mel yelled
at the top of her voice, "Get lost before we
throw a bucket of water over you!"

Henrietta looked daggers at Sam and
Mel. "Come on, girls," she said snottily to
her friends. "These idiots obviously can't
take a joke. And they'll just try to make
Vicki like them by telling her tales about us.
The babies! Come on, let's go back to our
comfy beds before they call her."

Henrietta and the rest of the ghosts quickly moved away from the barn, not wanting to get into trouble with Vicki. Camilla was trying to take the white sheet off her head as she ran across the yard, but the sheet got stuck and she stumbled and tripped over the feet of the girl in front of her. With some of the girls still covered in sheets and hanging onto each other, unable to see where they were going, Camilla's fall had a domino effect. The girls all toppled straight into the big muck heap. Henrietta, who'd been at the front of the ghostly gang, was lying right on the bottom!

The yard girls all burst out laughing.

"Yuk!" said Jess. "I bet that posh caravan stinks disgusting tonight!" she chuckled.

"Come and look, Car," said Amber.

Cara made her way shakily back over to the window. She did manage a small smile when she saw all the livery girls

covered in horse muck but her face was still
white with fear.

"I don't think I'll be able to sleep at all
now," she said.

"Honestly, babe, don't worry," Mel said,
putting her arm round the shivering Cara.
"I'll pull my hay bale right up to yours so
we can sleep next to each other. And we'll
get the puppies to sit at the end of your
bed like guard dogs."

"I'm not sure how good they'll be!" Cara managed another smile. "But I'll feel loads better if you're right there."

"No worries. It's only a stupid story anyway. Just keep thinking about Henrietta, Camilla and the rest of those idiots all covered in poo!"

Chapter 7

After a very late night and a string of scary dreams about galloping headless horses, Cara woke up feeling dull and tired. Sam bounced awake as if nothing had happened.

"Rise and shine, sleepy heads!" she yelled.

Mel yawned as she sat up and stretched her arms. "Are you ever quiet, Sam?" she mumbled.

Sam shook her head. "Only when I'm sleeping."

Amber, who had slept next to Sam, grinned. "You're not that quiet when you're sleeping – you snore like a pig!"

Laughing and teasing each other, the girls got dressed.

"I can't believe that after all I ate yesterday, I feel so hungry," giggled Darcy.

Jess pulled her T-shirt over her head. "So what's for breakfast?" she asked.

Cara, who was beginning to feel a bit more lively, rummaged around in their food bags. She looked up with a smile on her face. "How about bacon butties?"

As they fried strips of bacon in a pan perched on the little gas fire in the camping field, Vicki strolled by with Treasure and Hunt scampering at her heels. The smell of yummy sizzling bacon sent the pups into hyper-drive. They raced towards the hot frying pan and had to be held back by Cara before they jumped into it to gobble up the bacon.

"Don't be silly, you'll burn yourselves," she giggled.

Wriggling in Cara's arms, the pups licked her nose then started to pull at her hair.

"Did you get disturbed in the night?" Vicki asked.

The girls all looked at each other. Much as they hated Henrietta, they didn't really want to grass her up.

Jess shrugged. "Somebody might have been messing about in the yard," she said vaguely.

A slow smile spread across Vicki's face. "I think they might have had a collision with the muck heap — I only hope they have a good wash before they come to the gymkhana games!"

It was another lovely late August day. Some of the leaves on the trees were turning golden and a smell of ripe apples drifted across the fields from the orchard. Luckily the ponies weren't difficult to catch this morning, so the girls had plenty of time to give them a really good grooming. Cara spent a long time on Taffy, making sure there wasn't a single speck of mud on his beautiful creamy blond coat.

"You'll be the best-looking pony in the show," she said as she brushed him down.

Taffy tossed his head as if to say, Of course I will! Cara used a stable rubber to get a fine shine on his coat, then brushed his silky mane and tail with the dandy brush. She could tell Taffy was excited. He neighed at passing ponies and turned his head this way and that to see what was going on in the busy yard.

Ponies were being groomed everywhere – even Henrietta and Camilla were getting their hands dirty! Cara took a quick sideways glance to see how the posh girls were getting on. It made her smile to see Henrietta fumbling with the dandy brush and Camilla having trouble picking out Cleopatra's feet.

Sam was smiling too. "It's about time they worked up a sweat like the rest of us!" she giggled.

Mel winked as she tightened Candy's girths. "Hope the smell of the muck heap isn't too much for the poor ponies!"

In a happy mood, the girls trotted over to the biggest gymkhana field, which was already filling up with parents. Cara spotted her mum sitting between Mel's dad and two big brothers. Her heart lifted with happiness at the sight of her. She blew a kiss and waved across the field to her mum, who smiled and blew a kiss back.

"They look nice and cosy together," joked Mel.

Cara stared thoughtfully at Mel, who was fast becoming her best friend. Mel's mum had died when she was little, and her

dad and big brothers had brought Mel up.
When Cara heard that Mel only had one
parent, she had wanted to talk to her about
losing her dad but she'd always been too
shy. Maybe one day she would – it would
be good to talk to somebody other than her
mum about the dad she missed so much.

A loud neigh from Taffy stopped Cara
daydreaming. He was tossing his head
and pawing the ground as if to say, Get
a move on!

Jess was already mounted up. "We'd
better line up for the relay race," she said.
"It's starting in a few minutes."

Cara gave her friends the thumbs-up sign.
"Good luck!" she called out as they trotted off.

Watching from the side, Cara and Amber
could see from the determined expression on
all the competitors' faces that this was going
to be a tough race.

Henrietta had a confident smirk on her

face. "Don't worry about the pink team," she said to her friends. "They just got lucky yesterday. They're a load of rubbish really!"

One of them looked down her nose at the pink team, who were lined up beside them. "You can tell that from their ponies!" she scoffed.

Cara went red with anger. She was sick and tired of Henrietta's insults – and she'd had a bad night thanks to her stupid tricks. Forgetting her shyness, she shouted over to her friends. "Go for it, girls!"

Cara held her breath as Vicki waved a flag and the race started. Darcy had decided to go first this time, and she and Duke charged across the field and back in a blink.

Cara punched the air with excitement. "You're winning!" she yelled.

Jess followed Darcy, but Rose didn't like the crowds at all and was slow to start.

"Come on! Come on!" Cara whispered under her breath.

By the time Jess got back they'd slipped from first place to third.

Sam went next on Beanz, which cheered Cara up. If any pony could go at speed it was Beanz. But sadly he was a bit too fast. He charged along and wasted precious seconds by going past Mel before Sam could pass her the baton.

Eventually Mel got the baton and Cara watched her take off on lovely fleet-footed Candy. The pink team was now down to fourth place. Could they possibly win?

"Come on, Mel, you can do it," Cara called out.

Mel charged up the field, overtaking the blue and green teams, but she couldn't make up the lost time and Henrietta's snooty purple team came in first. Cara and Amber quickly joined their friends at the end of the race and tried to cheer them up.

"That was bad luck," said Cara.

Sam's normally smiley face fell into a glum expression. "It was my fault. Sorry, guys, I couldn't slow Beanz down."

Jess shook her head. "No, it was my fault. Rose was just so nervous."

"I can't believe we won the practice race yesterday but lost the real thing," said Darcy.

"I know winning isn't important but it's so annoying to lose to Henrietta," said Mel, biting her lip.

Cara gave her a smile. "Don't worry, Mel, it's the showjumping competition next and nobody's going to beat you at that."

Cara was right. Mel won the showjumping easily. Her brothers clapped and cheered when she went up to get her prize.

The next race was walk, trot and canter. Cara joined her friends at the line-up. With Amber and Mel behind her, she waited tensely for the starter's flag to fall, then pressed her heels into Taffy's side and set off at a brisk walk. It was hard to stop eager little Taffy from breaking into a trot but Cara held him on a tight rein, and like the good boy he was, Taffy obeyed her.

But when Cara turned to come back, she saw that Amber wasn't waiting for her as planned. Mel was there, mounted on Candy but holding onto Stella's reins – where was Amber? She was supposed to be doing the trotting bit of the race! As Cara got closer to the finishing line, she could see Mel shaking her head.

"Amber's not here. The strap on her hat broke. She's had to get another one. You'll have to trot for her," shouted Mel.

Cara went white but Mel just gave her a shove. "You'll be fine. Go, go, go!" she spluttered.

Cara quickly turned Taffy and, loosening his reins, allowed him to go into a brisk trot. Neighing with excitement, Taffy overtook Camilla on Cleopatra, who was on the other side of them. Grumpy Cleopatra snorted, and with a sharp jerk of her head she reached over and bit little Taffy on the neck. In a state of shock, Taffy shied, but Cara kept a tight hold on his reins.

"It's OK, sweetheart," she gasped.

Seeing Cleopatra reaching over to have another go, Cara glared at Camilla, who couldn't control her wild thoroughbred.

"Get her away from Taffy!" she screamed.

But it was too late. Cleopatra took a big bite at Taffy's neck, and this time the normally steady palomino bolted out of the ring. As he galloped across the field, Cara could feel her grip on him loosening. She lost control and tumbled to the ground, where she landed in a patch of thick mud.

As Cara struggled to her feet, wiping mud and tears from her face, her mum came running up, followed by Mel's dad and Vicki.

"Sweetheart! Are you all right?" her mum gasped.

Cara buried her head in her hands, then looked around wildly. "I shouldn't have lost my grip on Taffy's reins. Where is he?" she asked.

Mum put an arm around her shaking shoulders. "Don't worry, Susie went after him," she said soothingly.

"Are you OK?" asked Vicki. "Can you get up all right?"

"I'm fine," said Cara. "Nothing broken. I just feel well embarrassed."

"Well, don't be," said Vicki. "It wasn't your fault. If you're sure you're OK, I'm going back to have a word with Camilla. She really needs to get Cleopatra under control." And she walked back to the gymkhana field.

"That vicious Cleopatra!" Cara seethed.

Her mum nodded sympathetically. "We could see her laying into Taffy from where we were sitting," she said.

Cara wiped tears off her muddy face. "Camilla was useless," she said. "She couldn't even hold her!"

Mel's dad offered Cara a bottle of water, which she gulped down thirstily. "You'll be fine when you get your breath back," he said softly.

As they walked slowly back across the field, Mel and Amber came rushing over.

"I'm so sorry about leaving you like that," said Amber. "It was my hat . . ."

"I didn't mind standing in for you," said Cara. "We were doing just fine until Cleopatra started ripping holes in Taffy's neck."

Mel grinned at her. "Yeah, but thanks to mad Cleopatra, Vicki disqualified Henrietta's team from the race. Jess's team won."

Cara smiled for the first time since her tumble. "Good! I'm glad," she said.

★

Covered in mud, Cara went back to the gymkhana field with her mum, Mel

and Mel's dad. On the way they passed
Henrietta. She looked in disgust at Cara's
muddy jodhpurs. "She can't even handle
a scabby little palomino!" Her loud voice
carried halfway across the field.

Seeing poor Cara's heartbroken face,
Mel whirled round and glared at Henrietta.
"You're a nasty cow!"
she cried.

Her dad had
to restrain her
from running up
to Henrietta and
thumping her!

"Don't sink so low,
sweetheart, she's not worth it," he said, and
turning his back on shocked Henrietta, he
walked on past her.

Chapter 8

Henrietta's cruel comment completely
finished Cara off. "I feel so stupid," she said
over and over again.

Mel's dark eyes blazed. "You're *not* stupid,
Car, it's Henrietta who's the stupid one
– and Camilla for not being able to control
her mad pony," she said.

Cara shook her head.
"They're not the ones
who fell off in front of
all those people," she
wept.

Mel's dad gave her
a gentle pat on the arm.

"It's not the falling off that matters, it's the getting back on that counts."

Cara's face went very white. "I am *not* going back into that ring," she said through gritted teeth.

Her mum took hold of her hand. "You'll be all right, love, it's just nerves."

Cara's face was set. "No, Mum," she replied.

"But what about the other races?" Mel asked.

Cara nervously nibbled her fingernails. "I am not going back into that ring and that's final," she insisted.

There wasn't much time to argue as Mel, Jess, Darcy, Amber and Sam were all doing the potato race. Standing next to Taffy, Cara watched them race, and even in her sorry state, she smiled at their antics. The pink team had no trouble at all racing down the line to pop the potatoes into the bucket, but by the end of the race all the potatoes were once again in Beanz's belly!

Taffy tossed his head and neighed with excitement when he saw his best friends, Stella, Rose, Beanz, Duke and Candy having such fun. When he heard their shrill neighs, he pulled at his reins as if he wanted to join in too.

Cara gripped his reins tightly. "No, Taffy, we're not playing today," she said firmly.

Then something happened that brought tears to Cara's eyes. Taffy shook his pretty little head and sighed a big heavy sigh as if he was really sad. If he'd made a fuss, like tossing his head or pawing the ground, Cara might have ignored him. The fact that he just sighed sadly melted her heart. It hit her like a thunderbolt that she'd been so busy thinking of herself she'd forgotten how much Taffy loved gymkhana games.

Feeling ashamed of herself, she leaned forward and pressed her face into Taffy's silky blond mane. "Why should you miss out on all the fun just because I'm a wimp?" she whispered.

As she sniffed in the warm smell of Taffy, Cara recalled how her dad had taught her to ride her bike. She'd cried when she'd fallen off and cut her knee but her dad had popped her right back on.

"Come on, sweetheart, do this for me," he'd whispered in her ear.

Cara had gripped the handlebars as her dad pushed her off, and she'd managed to get her balance. Then, laughing with joy, she'd cycled right into a hedge, but at least she'd cycled! Her dad had picked her up and whooshed her high into the air.

"That's my brave girl!" he'd cried, then
hugged her tightly in his big strong arms.

Cara lifted her face out of Taffy's mane
and looked up at the blue sky overhead.

"I'm still your brave girl, Dad," she said, and pressing her heels into Taffy's side, she trotted into the ring to join her friends for the sack race!

The sight of Cara trotting towards them made Jess, Amber, Mel, Sam and Darcy cheer. Mel leaned across and flung an arm round Cara's shoulders.

"You total star!" she said.

Cara grinned at her smiling friends. "I couldn't let Taffy down, could I?" she told them.

They didn't win the sack race, but none of the pink team cared because they had the biggest laugh of the weekend doing it. Mel was so small she disappeared into the sack, Candy trotted over Amber's toes, while Beanz grabbed a sack in his mouth and tried to eat it! Cara fell over three times and Sam, who was hopping backwards, tripped Henrietta up! By the end of the race the girls were laughing themselves silly.

"I've never had so much fun in my life!" gasped Cara.

Then she quickly changed out of her muddy clothes because the next event was the one she'd pinned all her hopes on – best turned-out pony. As she scrambled into clean clothes, her friends groomed Taffy and gave his saddle and bridle a last-minute polish.

Mel cleaned Cara's boots, which had got

dusty during the sack race. "You've both got to be spotless for this event," she said.

Cara straightened her riding hat then quickly mounted up. "Let's show them, Taf!" she said, and the little pony neighed loudly as if to say, no problem!

Cara trotted into the ring, where she and the other competitors were examined from every angle. Cara was relieved when she saw that Camilla hadn't entered Cleopatra, but Henrietta was there. She looked immaculate but she ruined her image by fidgeting and complaining even though President had perfect manners in front of the judges.

Taffy was also a perfect gentlemen — he never fussed when his tail and mane were stroked but politely allowed the judges to feel his coat and check his feet. When the judges had finished with Taffy, they turned their attention to Cara, who sat up straight in the blazing sunshine looking cool and confident!

Finally the judges made up their minds and Vicki announced the result. "The winner for the best turned-out pony is Cara on Taffy," she called out.

Cara couldn't believe she was hearing right. She leaped out of the saddle and flung her arms round Taffy's neck. "You're the best pony in the world," she cried.

Taffy nodded his head and neighed happily as if he were agreeing with her!

With her friends cheering her on, and her mum and Mel's dad and big brothers waving at her, Cara trotted up to receive her first riding trophy. It was a model of a silver horse on a wooden base. As she took the trophy from Vicki, she kissed it, and that was the photograph her mum took of her. Later Cara framed it and placed it on her bedside table between the one of her smiling dad and the one of gorgeous Taffy.

After the presentation Cara's mum rushed up and hugged her. "Your dad would have been so proud of you, sweetheart," she said with tears in her eyes.

Laughing with joy, Cara threw her arms around her mum. "This has been the best weekend ever!" she said.

THE END

For fun, games and more information about
Vicki's Riding School log on to:
www.**katiesperfectponies**.co.uk

Here Comes the Bride

Katie Price's Perfect Ponies

Here Comes the Bride

Perhaps there was a way of looking after the ponies and seeing Vicki too...

Jess and her friends spend as much time as they can with their favourite ponies at Vicki's Riding School. When Vicki tells the girls she's going to be chief bridesmaid at her best friend's wedding, they plan a very special surprise for her...

But when the wedding day dawns, everything goes wrong – will the girls and their ponies get there in time?

Little Treasures

Little Treasures

"As long as you can ride a pony and follow clues, you'll be fine..."

With the girls and their ponies all performing so well at her riding school, Vicki challenges them to try something different – a charity treasure hunt! All the girls are excited and hoping to win.

But snooty livery girl Henrietta is also desperate to come first, and when Cara and Mel find some surprise treasure during the hunt, it looks like she might just do that...

3

Katie Price's
Perfect Ponies

Fancy
Dress
Ponies

Fancy
Dress
Ponies

Sam and her mum left the clown costume hanging over the stall and hurried to the tack room. They had no idea that someone had been listening in ...

It's the start of the summer holidays, and Sam and her friends are looking forward to spending as much time as they can at the stables. They decide to take part in a fancy dress competition, and work hard making themselves and their ponies look gorgeous.

But, as usual, stuck-up Henrietta is determined to spoil their fun. Is dressing up such a good idea after all ...?